MONSTER By Mistake!

Monster by Mistake

Adapted by **Mark Mayerson**

Edited by **Paul Kropp**

Based on the screenplay by
Mark Mayerson *and* **Kim Davidson**

Graphics by **Studio 345**

WINDING
STAIR
PRESS

Monster By Mistake
Theme Song

Hi my name is Warren and I'm just
a kid like you,

Or I was until I found evil
Gorgool's magic Jewel.

Then he tricked me and I read
a spell, now every
time I sneeze,

Monster By
Mistake…

My sister Tracy tries the
Spell Book. She
never gets it right.

But Tracy doesn't ever give
up, 'cause you know one day
she might

Find the words that will
return me to my former width
and height.

I'm a Monster By Mista….ah….ah…

I'm gonna tell you 'bout Johnny the ghost,

He's a wisecracking, trumpet playing friend.

He lives up in the attic (shhh…Mom and Dad don't know)

Johnny always has a helping hand to lend.

My secret Monster-iffic life always keeps me on the run.

And I have a funny feeling that the story's just begun.

Everybody thinks it's pretty awesome I've become

A Monster By Mistake!

I'm a Monster By Mistake!

I'm a Monster By Mistake!

Monster by Mistake
Text © 2002 by Winding Stair
Graphics © 2002 by Monster by Mistake Enterprises Ltd.
Monster By Mistake Created by Mark Mayerson
Produced by Cambium Entertainment Corp. and Catapult Productions
Series Executive Producers: Arnie Zipursky and Kim Davidson

National Library of Canada Cataloging in Publication Data

Mayerson, Mark
      Monster by mistake

(Monster by mistake ; 1)
Based on an episode of the television program, Monster by mistake.
ISBN 1-55366-210-5

I. Davidson, Kim II. Kropp, Paul, 1948- III. Cambium Film & Video
Productions Ltd. IV. Monster by mistake (Television program) V. Title.
VI. Series: Mayerson, Mark Monster by mistake ; 1.

PS8576.A8685M66 2002   jC813'.6   C2002901101-9
PZ7.M39M66 2002

Winding Stair Press
An imprint of Stewart House Publishing Inc.
290 North Queen Street, #210
Etobicoke, Ontario, M9C 5K4 Canada
1-866-574-6873

Executive Vice President and Publisher: Ken Proctor
Director of Publishing and Product Acquisition: Susan Jasper
Production Manager: Ruth Bradley-St-Cyr
Copy Editing: Martha Campbell
Text Design: Laura Brady
Cover Design: Darrin Laframboise

This book is available at special discounts for bulk purchases by
groups or organizations for sales promotions, premiums, fundraising
and educational purposes. For details, contact: Stewart House
Publishing Inc., Special Sales Department, 195 Allstate Parkway,
Markham, Ontario L3R 4T8. Toll free 1-866-474-3478.

1 2 3 4 5 6   07 06 05 04 03 02

Printed and bound in Canada by Champlain Graphics Inc.

COLLECT THEM ALL

8 BOOKS SO FAR!

Contents

Chapter 1

The old Amberson house sat high on a hill looking down on the rest of the town. Many years ago a rich family had lived there, but now the old house was falling apart. Its wood was rotting, its paint was peeling, and many of its windows were broken. Everyone in town thought the house was empty, but everyone can sometimes be wrong.

Way up in one of the upper rooms, there was a strange creature from another world. He was tiny and blue, with pointed ears and a horn growing out of his forehead.

The creature was called Gorgool. Before coming to Earth, he was a being of great power – a prince. But now Gorgool was trapped inside a clear ball that was no bigger than a soccer ball. He paced and fumed and rolled around the old house, but could not get out of the ball. As you might expect, this did not make Gorgool happy.

"My day is coming. I can feel it!" he muttered to himself. "Those who conquered me will soon be conquered. Then the whole universe will bow before the power of Gorgool!"

He shook his fist angrily at the empty room.

"But first I have to break the spell that keeps me trapped in here." Gorgool looked around in frustration, then called for his servant. "Idiot! Imbecile! Where are you?"

Gorgool's servant was not named

Idiot or Imbecile. But he was not terribly bright. He could tell by his master's voice that Gorgool was angry. Quickly he came running into the room and bowed before Gorgool.

"Master, good news! I have found the *Book of Spells*!"

"Excellent!" Gorgool chuckled. "Get the Jewel of Fenrath. Then read the spell that will set me free!"

"And then I'll be rewarded, won't I, Master?" the servant begged.

"Only when you get me out of here, you wretched imbecile! Now get the jewel!"

The servant went off to the next room and picked up the magical Jewel of Fenrath.

The jewel had come through the vortex with Gorgool months ago. Now it felt cold in the servant's hands, and that made it hard for him to hold. In fact, he was holding the jewel so carefully that he didn't see the pile of wood boards on the floor ahead of him.

"Ooooh," he shouted as he tripped on the wood and flipped forward. "Oh no!" he screamed as the jewel went flying out of his hands. "Oh my!" he cried as the jewel bounced on the windowsill and out the window.

The servant could only stare helplessly as the jewel fell from the porch roof and

tumbled down the hill. And there was really nothing he could do when the Jewel of Fenrath bounced into the back of a pickup truck driving down the street. In seconds, the jewel was gone!

The servant groaned.

Somehow he had to explain all this to Gorgool. He almost crawled as he went into the room where Gorgool was waiting, expecting to be set free.

"Ah, you're back! Where is the jewel?"

He felt so foolish. "Master . . . the jewel . . . it's gone!"

"Gone?" Gorgool shouted.

"It fell and bounced and . . . and . . . and now it's in the back of a truck," the servant cried.

"Imbecile! Idiot! How could you lose the Jewel of Fenrath?" Gorgool screamed. "Find it now! Immediately!"

Chapter 2

Johnny B. Dead, the ghost who haunted the old Amberson house, was happy to be home. He had just returned from a fine vacation at the beach, but was feeling a little tired from his trip.

As a ghost, Johnny didn't have to worry about plane tickets and rental cars; he simply flew to a good hotel and went daily to the beach.

"Didn't get much of a tan," he said to himself, as he approached his home. "But I guess a ghost with a suntan would be a little strange."

Just as Johnny reached the porch with his suitcase, Gorgool's servant came charging out the front door. The door slammed open and right through Johnny.

"Hmm. Looks like I've got some uninvited houseguests. I better check this out," Johnny said to himself.

The ghost flew through the house, inspecting each of the rooms. There was a little leftover porridge in the kitchen, a broken chair in the living room and a messed-up bed on the second floor.

Just like Goldilocks, Johnny thought. He wondered who might be sleeping in his bed!

Johnny kept searching through the rooms until he came upon the little blue creature in the ball.

"Well, well," said Johnny. "Who might you be?"

"I am Gorgool," the creature announced. His voice was very powerful for a creature about the same size as Johnny's nose.

"That's kind of an unusual name, don't you think?" Johnny said. "Ever think of changing it to something simpler, like Ralph or Fred?"

"Don't insult me, ghost."

The ghost tipped his hat. "My name's Johnny. Johnny B. Dead, if you want to be formal."

"Put me down or you will pay! No one disobeys the mighty Gorgool!" he threatened.

Johnny was usually quite kind to strangers, but he didn't like the attitude of this noisy blue creature. "Well, Mr. Gorgonzola or whatever your name is. I don't know what you are or where you

came from, but I think you've got a bit of an attitude problem. I suggest you leave."

"I will be happy to leave this slum," replied Gorgool, looking around with distaste. "I am simply waiting for my servant to return with the Jewel of Fenrath. Then he'll cast the spell that will free me from this wretched ball."

"Magic spell?" Johnny replied. "Not in my house! It's bad enough we've got a ghost in here," declared Johnny. "Listen, I've got some things to do around town. But when I get back, I expect you and that servant of yours to be gone."

Gorgool was speechless. No one in the universe dared to give an order to him – but this ghost was telling him to leave!

Johnny put down the ball and tipped his hat politely. "I wish I could say it's been a pleasure meeting you, Mr. Gargoyle."

Gorgool grew even angrier when Johnny got his name wrong a second time. Still, he said nothing until Johnny had flown off. Then he muttered the words of his revenge: "You will regret this after I'm free!"

Chapter 3

Warren Patterson was not an impressive-looking kid. He had yellow hair, stick-out ears and eyes that seemed to bug out of his head. In fact, Warren was the last person you might expect to do battle with Gorgool, the mighty ruler of Fenrath. But Warren would end up surprising even himself as the day wore on.

Warren had just received a wonderful present – a remote-control toy car. He was busy steering his toy car down the sidewalk when a pickup truck drove past.

"Ah-choo," sneezed Warren. He was very allergic to dust and pollen.

In this case, the dust came from the pickup truck hitting a pothole in the street. The pothole caused the rear of the truck to bounce. And the bounce knocked the Jewel of Fenrath out of the truck and onto the sidewalk.

Warren's remote-control car drove right into it.

Warren came running up. He picked up the jewel and examined it. What's this thing? Warren wondered as he turned the jewel around in his hand.

Suddenly, he realized that his toy car had kept going. Warren put the jewel in his jacket pocket and took off after the car.

When Warren got to the end of the block, he saw the worst thing he could imagine – Billy Castleman had his car!

Billy Castleman had been picking on Warren for the last eight years. He would probably have picked on Warren even longer except for the fact that Warren was only eight years old.

"Look at this great car I found," sneered Billy. "Just the kind of car I always wanted."

"It's mine, Billy," said Warren quietly.

"Oh yeah?" said Billy, raising his voice. "Prove it!"

"I have the controller," replied Warren.

Billy smiled. He held out the car to Warren as if he were giving it back. "Okay. You can have it . . . if you can take it away from me," taunted Billy.

Warren wanted his car back, but knew that it would be useless to take on Billy Castleman. He wouldn't stand a chance. "I don't want to fight," Warren said.

"That's too bad," replied Billy, "because I DO!"

Billy pushed Warren to the ground and the controller fell out of Warren's hand. Billy picked it up.

"Now I've got the car AND the controller," he said with a nasty smile. "So long, Warren. I'll bring the car back when the batteries get worn out."

Billy stomped off and Warren got up,

feeling terrible. The car was his favorite toy and now it was gone. What would he tell his parents? How could he ever get it back?

At that moment, Warren's sister, Tracy, arrived. "Warren, I've been looking for you," she said. "It's time to go home."

Warren didn't say anything. He stood there, feeling dumb and powerless.

"Hey, where's your toy car?" Tracy asked. "I thought you were playing with it when you left the house."

"Billy Castleman's got it," said Warren quietly.

"What?" exclaimed Tracy. "You let him take your new car? When are you going to stand up to him?"

Warren didn't answer. He had been asking himself that same question for as long as he could remember. Someday, he kept saying to himself, I'll teach Billy a lesson. But when would that day ever come?

"Where's Billy gone?" demanded Tracy. "There's no way I'm going to let that bully steal your car."

Chapter 4

Billy Castleman was strolling down the street when he heard Tracy yelling.

"Come back here, Billy Castleman! We want that car back!"

Billy saw the determined look on Tracy's face. While her brother, Warren, might be a pushover, Tracy Patterson

never gave up. If he wanted to keep the car, he had to get moving.

Up ahead was the old Amberson house. It would be the perfect way for him to get away from Tracy and Warren. They'd be too chicken to follow me into a haunted house, thought Billy, as he ducked inside.

Warren and Tracy got to the stairs of the house. "We can't go in there. Everybody says the Amberson place is haunted," said Warren.

"You want your car back, don't you?" asked Tracy.

"Yes," Warren replied.

"Then stop acting so scared and stay close behind me. We're going in!"

Tracy slowly opened the door to the house. Warren peeked in from behind her. The living room was old and dusty. There were cobwebs and bugs everywhere. Billy was nowhere in sight.

"I d-d-don't think he's in here," said Warren. "Let's g-g-go home."

Tracy motioned for Warren to be quiet. Silently, she gestured that they should go up the stairs. She expected to find Billy hiding up there.

What Tracy didn't know was that Billy had already left the house. The only being on the second floor was Gorgool, who was waiting impatiently for his servant to return with the jewel. The ruler of Fenrath wanted to be free from the clear ball that trapped him. He wanted to be gone from this dusty old house and the stupid ghost who couldn't get his name right.

As Warren and Tracy looked around the upstairs room, something started to glow. "What's that light?" asked Tracy.

Warren realized that the glow was coming from his pocket. He took out the jewel and showed it to his sister. "I forgot.

I found this on the street a few blocks from here," said Warren.

Hidden in his corner, Gorgool couldn't believe his eyes. That boy had the Jewel of Fenrath, the jewel that would set him free! Quickly, he formed a plan.

"Oh, children, please help me!" Gorgool begged in the voice of an old man.

Tracy and Warren turned in the direction of Gorgool's voice. They were astounded to see a little blue man in a ball.

"Who . . . I mean, what are you?" asked Tracy.

"My name is Gorgool and I'm a . . . a magical elf," Gorgool told them. He was making up the story as he went along. "A wicked magician cast a spell on me and trapped me in this ball," he said as sweetly as he could. "You can free me if you just read something from that book over there."

"L-l-let's get out of here," begged Warren.

Gorgool couldn't let them get away, so he tried again. "Please free me," he begged. "If I don't get out of here soon, I'll die!" Gorgool coughed a couple of times for effect.

"We can't just leave him here," said Tracy. "Just read the stuff from the book and then we'll go. I mean, it can't hurt to help him, can it?"

Warren handed Tracy the jewel and headed over to the book. It was a really ancient book, wrapped in leather. Warren didn't understand any of the words, but figured he could sound them out.

Carefully he brushed some dust off the page and began. *"Ick flenum bar grish-nak pon stimoy,"* he read.

No one but Gorgool saw that the jewel in Tracy's hand had begun to glow. Gorgool waited anxiously for Warren to finish reading the spell. He was about to be free!

The dust from the page swirled around Warren's head as he continued reading. *"Flan klartroph splin . . . har . . . har . . .ah . . . ah . . . ah-choo!"*

Warren sneezed before he could finish the spell.

Blue sparks came shooting out of the Jewel of Fenrath. Tracy was scared. She dropped the jewel to the floor. Then a slash of blue lightning came out of the jewel and hit Warren, lifting him off the floor.

Tracy was horrified! What was happening to her brother? What had this little blue man made them do?

Finally, the lightning stopped and Warren dropped to the floor. Tracy ran up to him. "Are you all right?" she asked. Warren was shaken, but seemed to be okay.

Gorgool, however, was not okay. He was angry. He was even angrier than he had been at the ghost.

"You fools!" Gorgool shouted. "You stupid incompetents! You clumsy brats! You've ruined the spell! Read it again so I can be free of this accursed ball!"

Warren and Tracy turned to see an angry, threatening Gorgool. This was not the nice little blue man who had asked them for help. This was the nasty ruler of Fenrath!

Tracy did the smart thing. She grabbed the jewel and her brother. Then she ran from the house.

Moments later, the slow-witted servant stumbled up the steps to Gorgool. "Master, I have failed," he sighed. "I looked and looked, but I couldn't find the jewel," he said. "It must have disappeared from the face of the Earth."

"Idiot! Imbecile! Did you see those children?" demanded Gorgool.

"Children?" asked the servant. "What children?"

"The girl and boy, you nitwit," yelled Gorgool. "They're the ones with the jewel! Now go after them and get it back!"

Chapter 5

Warren's sister kept lecturing him as they headed home.

"You have to get your car back from Billy Castleman," said Tracy. "He's a bully. The only way to handle a bully is to stand up to him. You've got to tell him that you want that car back."

"I can't," said Warren. "I'm afraid he's going to beat me up."

"He's not as tough as you think," said Tracy. "Bullies are all weak inside."

"Yeah, but I'm weak outside," Warren complained. "I'm just an ordinary kid with a . . . ah . . . ah . . . ah-choo!"

Tracy shook her head. "You could at least say 'excuse . . .'"

Her words dropped off. Her mouth fell open. Tracy couldn't believe what was in front of her.

Warren, her little brother, wasn't there any more. In his place was a giant blue monster that was still talking in Warren's voice.

" . . . you see, Billy's bigger than me. He could pound me to peanut butter, Tracy. I mean, what am I supposed to do about that?"

Tracy was speechless. She stared help-lessly at the monster with Warren's voice.

"W-w-w. . . ." Tracy couldn't even say

her brother's name. All she could do was point in his direction.

The Monster turned around, wondering what Tracy was pointing at.

"What?" asked the Monster.

Suddenly, the Monster looked down and noticed his own arm. Then he looked at his other arm. And then he saw the rest of his body.

"Aiiiieee!" he screamed. "I'm a monster! I'm all ugly! I'm a monster! Help! Help me!"

The large blue monster with Warren's voice kept yelling and running around in a panic. He seemed to be afraid of everything – including himself!

Tracy took a moment to gather her thoughts.

"We were talking," she muttered to herself. "Everything was fine. What happened? I think Warren sneezed. Yes! He definitely sneezed and then there was this monster guy. But he's got Warren's voice. Aha! I've got it!"

Tracy went to a nearby bush and grabbed a handful of dirt. When the frantic monster ran near her, she tossed the dirt in his face. He stopped in his tracks.

"What are you doing?" the Monster cried. "I need help! Don't throw dirt in my fah . . . fah . . . ah . . . ah . . . ah-choo!"

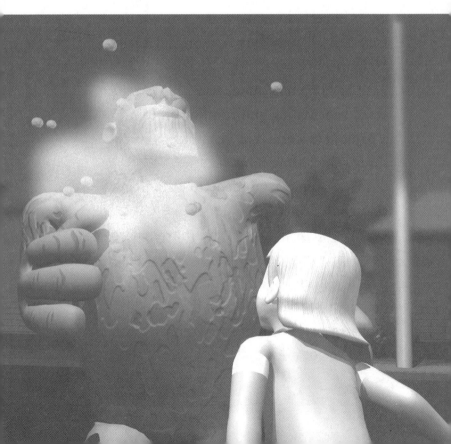

The Monster sneezed. In a flash, he changed back into Warren.

"It WAS the sneeze!" declared Tracy. "Just as I thought."

"What's going on?" asked Warren. "A second ago I was a big blue thing, and now I'm me, and. . . ." Warren was very confused. "Tracy, I don't understand any of this."

Tracy did. She took the jewel out of her pocket and held it out to her brother. "Warren," she said, "this is some kind of magic jewel. Somehow your sneeze got mixed up in that spell you read for the little blue guy. Now when you sneeze, you turn into a monster!"

"But I sneeze all the time because of my allergies," moaned Warren. "And I don't want to be a monster!" Warren was very upset, and with very good reason.

Tracy tried to cheer him up. "If a spell in that book did this to you," said Tracy, "there's probably a spell in the book that will fix it. We just have to go back and get the book."

"I don't want to go back there," said Warren. "That Gorgool guy gives me the creeps!"

"Warren, you've got to. Otherwise you'll turn into the monster over and over again. People will hate you. Look what happened to Frankenstein."

"Frank who?"

"Oh, never mind," Tracy told him. "Trust me, Warren. We've got to find a way to break this spell. The way to do it is back in the Amberson house. We've got to risk it. It's your only chance!"

Chapter 6

Warren and Tracy were almost back at the old Amberson house when Warren's toy car came zooming by.

"Hey! That's my car!" said Warren. He started running after it, zigging and zagging until he was halfway down the block.

That's when Billy Castleman walked up to Tracy. He was holding the car's controller.

"What's the matter?" asked Billy, with a sneer on his face. "Is your chicken brother running away from me?"

Tracy wasn't the least bit afraid of Billy Castleman. She knew the best way to deal with a bully was to tell him exactly what you want. "We want the car back, Billy!" said Tracy, looking determined.

"Really?" Billy asked. "It's not that nice a toy car."

"It's the best car my brother ever had. Now give it back," Tracy ordered.

"Well, I guess," Billy said. He twisted the controls and expected to see the car come zooming back. But nothing happened. Looking down the street, he could see that Warren had picked up the car.

"Hey, gimme that back!" he yelled at Warren.

Warren panicked. He saw Billy

– the biggest, toughest guy in his school –
coming after him. Warren took off. He
clutched the car to his chest and ran like
crazy down the street.

Billy wasn't ready to let Warren have
his car, so he ran after him.

And Tracy ran after both of them.
"Leave my brother alone!" she yelled.

The three kids began a chase scene
like in an old-time movie. Warren ran
past a garbage can and tipped it over as he
passed. Billy tripped on the can and fell
to the ground. Warren ran into a yard and
slammed the wooden gate in Billy's path.
Billy crashed into it and fell backwards.
Warren had gained a little time, but Billy
was getting really mad!

Warren looked frantically around the
yard. He had to hide, but where? There!
Inside the tool shed! If he was quiet,
maybe Billy wouldn't find him.

Billy got free of the gate and came
into the yard. He looked around carefully

for Warren. Had that little wimp gotten away? Was he hiding?

"Ah . . . ah . . . ah-choo!"

Billy heard the sneeze coming from the tool shed and he smiled. "I know where you are, Warren. This time, you're really going to get it!" Billy marched up to the shed and threw open the doors.

Warren's eyes were shut tight. He was ready for the worst beating of his

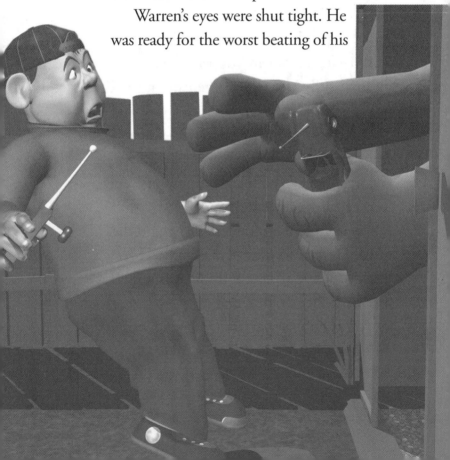

life. But nothing came. Why hadn't Billy hit him yet?

He opened his eyes to see Billy looking very scared. Billy also seemed a lot shorter than usual, almost like he had shrunk.

Tada! He remembered what sneezing did to him. He knew that Billy wasn't looking at Warren the weakling, he was staring at a giant blue monster!

Serves you right, the Monster thought, as he reached out his hands to grab Billy.

"Yiiiii!" Billy Castleman yelled. In sheer panic, he dropped the controller and ran for his life.

When Tracy reached the yard, it was all over. She saw her brother, the Monster, triumphantly holding his car and the controller.

"I got them back," said the Monster, smiling, "and I scared Billy Castleman! You know, Tracy, maybe being a monster isn't such a bad thing!"

"Well, I'm glad you got them back," said Tracy. "But being a monster is going to be a bit of a problem for you. Like sneezing in school. What do you think Ms. Gish will say when she sees a blue monster sitting in your desk?"

"Maybe 'help'?" the Monster suggested.

"More likely she'll call the police, or the zookeepers, or Mom. I don't know which would be the worst." Tracy stood there, thinking about the problem. "Warren, we've got to get you fixed. We've got to do something about this magic spell."

"Can't I scare Billy one more time, first?" asked the Monster. Suddenly he sneezed, turning back into Warren Patterson. "Rats!" said Warren. "No use chasing Billy now."

"Come on," said Tracy. "Let's go back to the Amberson place and get that book!"

Chapter 7

Johnny B. Dead was holding a shiny trumpet when he returned from his errands to the Amberson house. "They sure did a nice job cleaning up my old horn. It looks practically new."

Johnny plopped himself down in an easy chair, but was inspired by his trumpet. He jumped up. "Let's see how this baby sounds," he said and started playing a jazzy tune. Back when he was still alive, Johnny had been a pretty good jazz trumpeter. Even as a ghost, he could still blow a mean trumpet.

As Warren and Tracy approached the Amberson house, it was the trumpet that they heard.

"What's that?" asked Warren.

"I think it's an old song called *Smoke Gets in Your Eyes.*"

"That's not what I mean!" Warren told his sister. "I mean, there's somebody playing a trumpet in the Amberson house. But nobody's lived here for years!"

"Well, I don't think it's that blue guy

in the ball. He didn't strike me as the musical type."

"Maybe it's a ghost!" said Warren.

Tracy humphed as she sometimes did when she thought her brother was being silly. "I don't believe in ghosts," she told him.

"How about magic jewels and sneezing monsters?" asked Warren.

This caused Tracy to pause, but she quickly regained her nerve. "Even if it is a ghost, we still have to get the *Book of Spells*. You can't keep sneezing yourself into a monster every time your nose itches."

Warren knew there was no sense arguing with his older sister. He followed behind her as she entered the house.

Johnny heard the creaking of the door. "More intruders!" he said. He blew some loud notes on his horn, hoping to scare the new intruders away.

Warren was frightened. "Let's go home!

The ghost isn't even playing a tune any more," he pleaded.

"No!" Tracy told him firmly. "We've got to find that book!"

Johnny could tell that his scary horn playing hadn't worked. The kids were still coming into the house.

"Guess I'd better use the tried-and-true," he sighed. Johnny flew out of his chair and charged at the children, yelling his loudest BOO!

Warren and Tracy were shocked. A ghost! A real ghost. Warren started shaking and collapsed onto the floor.

"Just my luck," muttered Johnny. "He's a fainter, not a runner."

Tracy knelt down beside her brother. "Warren, are you okay?" Slowly Warren began to wake up. The first thing he saw was Johnny's horn.

"Is that a trumpet?" he asked, still a little dizzy.

This caught Johnny off guard. "Well, it isn't a baby trombone. Do you play?"

"A little," said Warren.

"Let's hear what you've got," said Johnny, handing the trumpet over to Warren.

Tracy couldn't help thinking how crazy everything was. Gorgool, the magic spell, the monster. And now Warren was playing trumpet for a ghost! What happened to that sensible world of just yesterday?

"I'm just a beginner," Warren said, as he started to blow the trumpet.

That was an understatement. If there was a melody in the noise, Johnny couldn't find it. "Ooh," said Johnny. "You need lessons. And maybe a new pair of lips."

"Sorry," sighed Warren. "I guess I need to practice more."

Johnny could see that he had hurt Warren's feelings. He put his arm around Warren to make him feel better. "Listen, kid, everybody sounds like that when they first start," Johnny said. "You'll get better."

"That's right, Warren. Don't get discouraged," Tracy added.

"And what are you kids doing here anyway? Nobody comes to this old place because they're scared of, well, me."

"Well, you're not so scary," Tracy told him. "And we've got a problem. We've got to get a book from upstairs so my brother won't turn into a monster any more," explained Tracy. "You see, the blue jewel zapped my brother when Gorgool . . ."

"Gorgool!" yelled Johnny. "I knew that guy was trouble! You kids wait here. Just leave it to me and I'll get things straight around here!"

Chapter 8

Johnny flew into Gorgool's room in a fury. This tiny blue intruder was nothing but trouble. He was making spells and turning kids into monsters. If this kept

up, Gorgool might turn Johnny's trumpet into a tuba. Or worse.

"I thought I told you to get out!" exclaimed Johnny.

"I'll go when I'm ready," argued Gorgool. "And I'm not quite ready."

This was too much for Johnny. "Listen, you pygmy porcupine, I'm the landlord here and you are hereby evicted!" Johnny's ghostly finger poked Gorgool through the ball for emphasis.

Gorgool stabbed Johnny's finger with the horn on his head.

"Ow!" yelled Johnny, as he pulled his finger out. But it was too late. A strange feeling started in Johnny's finger and began creeping up his arm. Soon, his head felt funny. "Uh oh," said Johnny in a shaky voice. "I don't feel so good."

Moments later, Johnny collapsed on the floor with his trumpet at his side.

Warren and Tracy were still waiting downstairs. "I don't hear the ghost any more," said Warren. "Maybe Gorgool got him, too. Tracy, we'd better get out of here."

"We have to get that book," said Tracy, "ghost or no ghost." She started up the stairs. Warren wasn't sure whether to follow his sister or not. The idea of going the other way, out the front door, seemed very appealing.

But suddenly, the front door opened. It was Gorgool's servant. The two of them stared at each other, both amazed.

"It's the children! They're here!" the servant said, somewhat stupidly. Then he grabbed Warren by the shoulder. "Where's the jewel?" he demanded.

"I haven't got it!" cried Warren.

The servant saw Tracy trying to sneak up the stairs. "Give me that jewel!" he yelled.

Tracy had never seen this man before. How did he know about the jewel? She decided to play dumb. "What jewel?" she asked.

The servant was in no mood to play games. "Give me the jewel or I'll hurt the boy!" he growled. He tightened his grip on Warren, who yelled in pain.

Tracy knew she had no choice. She took the Jewel of Fenrath out of her

pocket and brought it down to the servant. "Sit over there by the stairs," he barked.

Tracy walked over to the banister at the bottom of the stairs. The servant dragged Warren there and tossed him onto the floor.

"What are you going to do with us?" asked Tracy, as the servant approached them holding a rope.

"That's up to the boss," the servant told them. "But whatever it is, it won't be pretty."

Gorgool's servant tied up the two children. Then he took the jewel and went bounding up the stairs. He was thrilled. For once he'd actually been successful at following orders.

"Gorgool, I have it! I have the jewel! At last, you can be free!"

Chapter 9

As she sat tied up in the Amberson house, Tracy thought about everything that happened that day. "I'm sorry, Warren," she said. "If I hadn't told you to read from that book, none of this would have happened."

"It's not your fault," said Warren. "I shouldn't have let Billy Castleman take my car."

"I'm older than you," said Tracy. "I should have looked after you better."

"You keep telling me that I have to look after myself," said Warren. "You're right. But I guess it's too late to learn that lesson now. I wonder what they're going to do to us."

Both of the children wondered about Johnny. If not even a ghost had been able to deal with Gorgool, what chance could they possibly have?

Suddenly, Tracy had an idea.

"Warren, you've got to sneeze!" she said.

"But I don't *have* to sneeze," replied her brother.

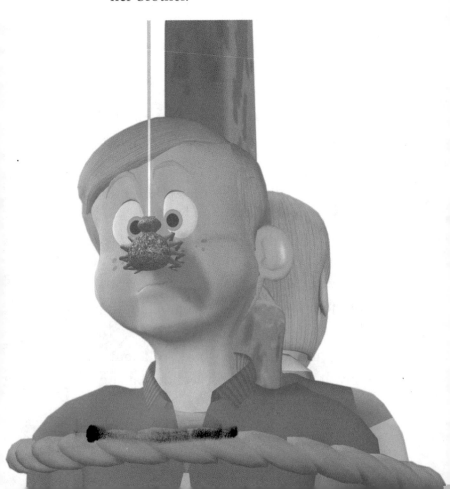

"I don't care about that. When you sneeze, you turn into that monster and you can break the ropes. So all you have to do is think about things that make you sneeze. Think about cats and dogs and . . ."

"Spiders!" yelled Warren.

"I didn't know you were allergic to spiders," said Tracy.

"I'm not. But there's a spider on my nose!" yelled Warren.

Warren tried to blow the spider off his nose, but the spider held on. Soon, Warren's nose began to twitch and itch. No question about it, he had to sneeze. "Ah . . . ah . . . ah-choo!"

In a flash, Warren turned into the Monster. His giant size was enough to break the ropes.

"You did it!" said Tracy. "Let's go!"

"But I'm not done!" the Monster cried, and then sneezed again. Immediately he was back to his normal self. The two children ran up the stairs.

In Gorgool's room, the servant was trying to find the spell that would free Gorgool. Unfortunately, the servant was not a very good reader. He was having a lot of trouble with the index.

"Ball? Clear ball? Now what would they call that spell?" the servant said out loud.

"Hurry, you fool!" screamed Gorgool.

The kids poked their heads in the door and peeked in. "Look," whispered Warren. "They knocked out the ghost!"

Tracy and Warren sneaked inside and hid behind a couch. Tracy found an old board on the floor, and she placed one end of it on the dresser where Gorgool stood. She left the other end on the ground.

Warren figured out the plan. He started driving his remote-control car up the board.

"Here it is! I found it!" said the servant.

"Then what are you waiting for? Read the spell!" yelled Gorgool.

The servant starting reading. *"Ick flenum bar grishnak pon stimoy,"* he read. He had to sound out each word, but it was working. As the words came out, the jewel started glowing.

Gorgool was grinning. He could almost taste his freedom. Then he'd get his revenge against everyone.

Suddenly, Gorgool noticed the car coming at him. His smile disap-peared

as he realized what was about to happen.

Bam! The toy car knocked Gorgool off the dresser. Gorgool and his sphere bounced around the room.

"Catch me!" cried Gorgool to his servant. "Save me!"

The servant stopped reading. As he went to rescue Gorgool, Warren and Tracy grabbed the book and jewel. Gorgool spotted the children.

"Stop them! Don't let them get away!" Gorgool yelled.

The servant put Gorgool on the table and started wrestling Tracy for the jewel. Tracy was determined, but she was no match for the giant servant. He grabbed the jewel from her, then threw her against the wall.

When Tracy hit, some ceiling beams from the old house fell in front of her. She was trapped.

Then the servant grabbed the book

from Warren and threw him onto the couch. A cloud of dust rose as Warren bounced on the cushions.

Chapter 10

"Quickly! Read the spell so I can be free!" yelled Gorgool.

His servant started to read again. *"Ick flenum bar grishnak pon stim . . .* is that *stimoy* or *stimwah* like in French?" he asked.

"It's *stimoy*, you idiot. Now quickly, finish the spell!"

As the servant was checking pronunciation, the couch dust made Warren sneeze, "Ah . . . ah . . . ah-choo!" and, of course, he turned into the Monster.

Now it was time for the Monster to stand up for his sister. Quickly, the Monster jumped, and the servant landed on the floor with the wind knocked out of him. The jewel and Gorgool both went flying.

Lightning from the jewel struck the air with a frightening sound. The new spell opened up a vortex that was like a vacuum cleaner. The vortex was sucking anything that was loose in the room.

Gorgool started to roll towards the vortex. "Noooo!" he screamed. "Catch me! Save me!"

The servant struggled to his feet. "I'm coming, Master!" he shouted. The servant dived and caught Gorgool, but the pull of the vortex was so strong that both of them were sucked into it!

Tracy and the Monster clutched at the fallen house beams. They kept holding on for their lives against the force of the vortex.

"Look!" yelled Tracy. "The book!" Some pages were coming loose and getting sucked into the vortex. Soon, the whole book was in the air. The Monster reached out and caught the *Book of Spells* before it was lost. He struggled back to Tracy, using all his strength.

The force of the vortex was incredible. It was pulling everything inside – furniture, the jewel, even Johnny the ghost.

"Oh no!" said the Monster. "We've got to save him!"

The Monster reached down and grabbed Johnny's trumpet. He blew the loudest note he could. It was the kind of note that people used to say would be loud enough to wake the dead. Sure enough, it worked.

Johnny woke up and looked around.

When he saw the vortex, he flew over to the kids. "Man the lifeboats! Ghosts and children first!"

The force of the vortex was too much for the old house. The ceiling fell in on Tracy and the Monster. The house's rotting timbers snapped. Windows broke and floors collapsed. The entire Amberson house shook, shuddered and fell to the ground with an ear-splitting crash!

Then everything was quiet.

Chapter 11

Nothing moved in the pile of rubble. All was still and silent.

Then, slowly, a piece of the roof started to shift. Finally, it got tossed aside by the Monster.

"Tracy! Are you all right?" asked the Monster.

Tracy's eyes opened and she sat up. "Ow! My head," she whimpered. "What happened?"

"The whole house fell down!" said the Monster. "But I've still got the book."

"What about the jewel?" asked Tracy.

"Here it is," said Johnny the ghost, who was sitting on a piece of the chimney. "I knew you kids needed it, so I saved it for you." He tossed the jewel to the Monster.

"Tracy, remember when the pages got sucked into the vortex. What if the spell we need is missing from the book? Do you think we'll ever find a way to stop me from turning into a monster?"

"I don't know," said Tracy. "Maybe one of the other spells will fix you up. We just need to be creative."

"Maybe you can find a spell to fix my house," muttered Johnny, looking at the rubble. "But you've got to be careful, kids. You never know what that jewel can do."

"All I know is that we better get home," said Tracy. "It's really late. Mom and Dad will be furious."

"At least you've got a home to go to," sighed Johnny. He picked up his battered trumpet and began a blues version of *Home Sweet Home*.

The Monster and his sister looked at each other. They felt badly about Johnny's house. In a way, they were responsible for what happened.

"Hey, Johnny. We've got an attic nobody ever uses," she said. "You're welcome to stay there, if you like."

"Won't you mind having a ghost for a tenant?" asked Johnny.

"I've already got a monster for a brother," said Tracy. "How could a ghost in the attic be any worse?"

"Besides, you can give me trumpet lessons!" said the Monster.

"Sounds like a fair deal! Thanks!" said a grateful Johnny.

They left the ruins of the Amberson place and headed towards home.

Not even a block away, Billy Castle-man was still prowling around. He was still angry that he had lost the toy car to Warren. And he really didn't understand where that monster had come from. Suddenly, he thought he heard Warren's voice.

The talking got nearer. Billy heard Warren saying, "I don't think I'll ever forget what happened tonight . . ."

Billy chuckled from his hiding place. From the sound of his voice, Billy knew his victim was walking right towards him. "The night's not over yet, Warren!" he whispered to himself.

Billy jumped out onto the sidewalk. He thought he was going to get another shot at little Warren Patterson, but there was that giant blue monster again! "W-w-warren?" asked Billy, his voice shaking.

"What's the matter, Billy?" asked the

Monster in Warren's voice. "You look like you've seen a ghost!"

Just then, Johnny the ghost popped out from behind the Monster. In a crazy voice, he asked, "Will you be my friend?"

This was all too much for Billy! He turned and ran as fast as he could. Halfway down the block, he tripped and fell headfirst into a garbage can. Then he scrambled to his feet, the garbage can still on his head.

"You see, Warren, there are some real advantages in being a monster," Tracy said. The others began laughing, and kept laughing all the way home.

The End

Visit the amazing
award-winning
MONSTER
By Mistake!
website

www.monsterbymistake.com

- ❏ experience a 3-D on line adventure
- ❏ preview the next episodes
- ❏ play lots of cool games
- ❏ join the MBM international fan club (it's free)
- ❏ test your knowledge with the trivia quiz
- ❏ visit a full library of audio and video clips
- ❏ enter exciting contests to win GREAT PRIZES
- ❏ surf in English or French

TOP SECRET!

Sneak Preview of New
Monster By Mistake Episodes

Even more all-new monster-iffic episodes of Monster by Mistake are on the way in 2003 and 2004! Here's an inside look at what's ahead for Warren, Tracy and Johnny:

- It promises to be a battle royale when a superstar wrestler comes to town and challenges the Monster to a match at the Pickford arena.
- There's a gorilla on the loose in Pickford, but where did it come from? It's up to the Monster, Tracy and Johnny to catch it and solve the mystery.
- When making deliveries for a bakery, Warren discovers who robbed the Pickford Savings and Loan. Can the Monster stop the robbers from getting away?
- Warren, Tracy and Johnny visit Fenrath, the home to Gorgool, the Book of Spells and the Jewel. In Fenrath, they discover who imprisoned Gorgool in the ball and what they must do in order to restore order to this magical kingdom.

MONSTER By Mistake! Videos

Six Monster by Mistake home videos are
available and more are on the way.

Each video contains
2 episodes and comes
with a special
Monster
surprise!

Only $9.99 each.

Monster by Mistake & Entertaining Orville
1-55366-130-3

Fossel Remains & Kidnapped 1-55366-131-1

Monster a Go-Go & Home Alone 1-55366-132-X

Billy Caves In & Tracy's Jacket 1-55366-202-4

Campsite Creeper & Johnny's Reunion
1-55366-201-6

Gorgools' Pet & Jungle Land
1-55366-200-8

About the people who brought you this book

Located in Toronto, Canada, **Cambium** has been producing quality family entertainment since 1982. Some of their best known shows are "Sharon Lois and Bram's The Elephant Show," "Eric's World," and of course, "Monster By Mistake"!

Catapult Productions in Toronto wants to entertain the whole world with computer animation. Now that we've entertained you, there are only 5 billion people to go!

Mark Mayerson grew up loving animated cartoons and now has a job making them. Monster By Mistake is the first TV show he created.

Paul Kropp is an author, editor and educator. His work includes young adult novels, novels for reluctant readers, and the bestselling *How to Make Your Child a Reader for Life*.